AF255528

AMERICA
LOOK WHAT YOU DID AGAIN !!!

Dear Georgia   May 9, 1944

My way of living has changed suddenly due to the fact of being shot down on one of our missions a while back. Am a P.O.W. now. We are allowed only one parcel each sixty days. Certain items are restricted. I wrote Mother a few days ago and informed her what I needed most. But I can receive any amount of letters. Would you please send me some photos of yourself. Say hello to your Mother and family. I wouder just

how long it will be before we can go bowling again. I hope by Christmas at least. We are allowed to write two letters and four cards, missing you, love
                Johnny

AMERICA
LOOK WHAT YOU DID AGAIN !!!

B . R .   R I N K E R

ReadersMagnet, LLC

1944 - Prisoner of World War II
Stalag Luft III in Sagan, Germany

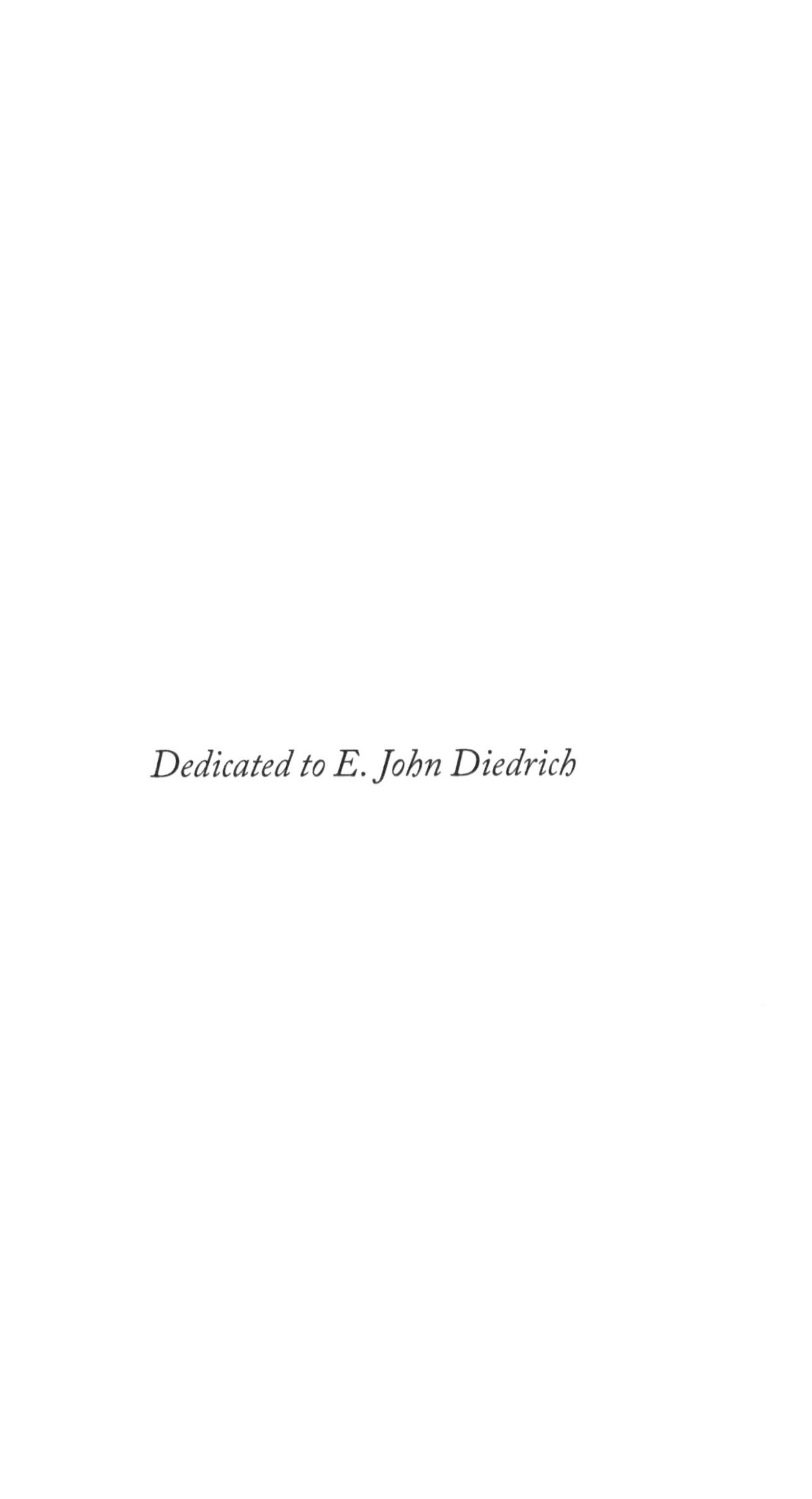

Dedicated to E. John Diedrich

As told by his love of 59 years
Georgia Diedrich

Acknowledgments

My greatest gratitude is for Georgia's excitement and willingness to share this piece of history and of her heart with me. Also, for Paul A. Diedrich, their son, who faithfully drove her to my salon regularly to add to her beauty and to write this true story.

Of course, we always drag our families into anything we do, so this is our "thank you" and dedication of this book to Johnny's bloodline and mine.

Edited by Daniel G. Diedrich
Cover by John Christian Jaksha
Computer Help: Matthew Joseph Jaksha
Collaborator: Renalyn Grego (Rain)
Georgia and John's family: Jon, Dan, Tad, Gigi, Paul
Grandchildren: Jeff, James, Julie, Joey, Jonathan, Jordan, Jenna, Nate, Daniel, Ted, Ben, Kate, Erin
Great Grandchildren: Kay-Leigh, Ana Jorga, Ava, Ian, Elija, Elle Jo, Cal

Regennia's family:
Matthew Joseph Jaksha and Lisa; Dillon's Family plus (Rivers)
Kirsten and Kelly Dow; Colton and Kaden
John Christian and Judy Jaksha; Jewel, Joy

"Did You Send the Snapshots Yet?"

Confined in this room, 20' × 20'
With nine other prisoners
Surrounded by 10,000 officers throughout camp
Our B-24 was shot down a while back
Can you send me photos of yourself?

Being called "Kriege" by Germans
Receiving one cup of barley soup
And one piece of dark bread daily
Playing bridge with our deck of cards
Don't forget your photo

Starting on a long winter march
The Russians are moving in
A 200 miles march to Nuremberg
Sneaking off to steal food from a pig pen
Did you send the snapshots yet?

Arriving in Nuremberg
People around me sick with pneumonia
Thinking I would be next to die
General George Patton came
"Boys, you're free. War's over."

The Red Cross came giving us food
One POW died from eating too much
Stepping on the Liberty Ship
Awaiting to see you face to face

By: Kate Lythgoe

2-2-09

Dearest Georgia,   November 13, 1944

Each letter from you, darling, definitely brings more and more happiness into my restricted life. My reason for craving snapshots so, is for present state of affairs, it is the closest we can be to one another. I hope the sisters won't be too angry with me for cluttering up their main parlor more than their want. What subjects have you taken up this semester? On my return to the states I intend to get my share of walking in the woods, skating, fishing, hunting, bowling, and dancing, if you wish, with you, Georgia, darling, to strains of beautiful, slow, sweet music. You'll have a big job teaching me all over again. I shouldn't be dreaming out loud. The parcel in which you enclosed your snapshots arrived on Oct. 26 in perfect shape. Thank you, Georgia you are as beautiful as ever. The one of you in the white suit makes me weak in the knees. You may write letters with envelopes if you wish. I'd prefer those to the forms, then you can enclose snapshots. Say hello to everyone maybe I'll be dropping in for a visit soon. Bye darling, thinking of you day and night. Don't practice bowling too much! Love Always, Johnny

Elmer John Diedrich, Jr.

Address: Avon, Minnesota.
Entered Service: March 17, 1943.
Branch of Service: Army Air Corps.
Trained: Sheppard Field, Texas; Buckley Field, Colorado; McKinley Field, Nevada; Clovis, New Mexico; Langley Field, Virginia; Morrison Field, Florida.
Overseas: March 21, 1944. Returned to U. S.: June 2, 1945.
Served in European Theatre.
Engagements: Eight missions over Germany, Bulgaria, Rumania, Yugoslavia.
Awarded: Air Medal, Good Conduct Medal, w/3 Battle Stars.
Discharged: Santa Anta, California, October 6, 1945.
Rank: Staff Sergeant. Served: 30½ months.
Present Occupation: Student, St. John's University, Senior
Shot down over Mostar, Yugoslavia, German prisoner of war over a year, liberated April 21, 1945 by Patton.

Georgia Veronica Schmid
Year Book Photo

At Johnny's request she sent this picture to him in Stalag Luft 3. He carried this photo in the window of his billfold for the rest of his life...fifty five years.

Name: Diedrich

Vorname: Elmer Jo hn

Dienstgrad: Sgt.

Erk.-Marke: 4047   OFLAG LUFT 3.

Serv.-Nr.: 37 555 539

Nationalität: U. S. A.

Baracke:

Raum:

K. Liebig, Hayen

Georgia

For the college book during Johnny and Georgia's courtship.

Georgia

Honeymoon happiness at Lake Superior

Hello to Georgia! & all the family!

What a thrill we got in the mail this evening — I enjoyed our surprise from you much more than the Presidential Debates on T.V.!!

Both of us were touched you thought of us with your very special book. We plan to read it so carefully so we can feel & understand the entire story of Jan's WW2 mission & imprisonment. He talked about so little those times we were together so this will bring Jan's life in focus for us. We did not know the military man or the banker, but knew the neighbor & the father, & friend.

And kudos to you for taking the time (& energy!) to do this special effort for Jan & family & friends.

After Sam & I read & remember with your pages, I'm going to

Georgia,
I Loved the book...It has helped me make a decision to do an action at Work. I thoroughly relaxed after reading your book Sunday after the hot mineral bath.   Your buddy, Judy
Thanks again for the Gift.

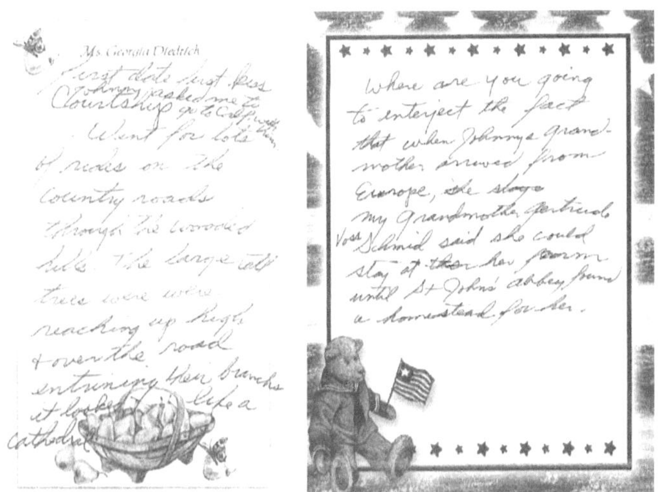

Dear Grandma Georgia & Paul,

Thank you so much for the twenty dollars. I was able to buy some awesome new speakers for my car. They sound amazing, it was a huge improvement from my other speakers.

My mom was really excited about her cd player, and I was able to install it for her on christmas eve. She was able to listen to the entire eagles cd collection that I got her for christmas.

School is going great for me I finished yet another semester. I can't wait to start my business classes this semester. Well I hope things are going great down there in New Mexico.

Love,
Ben

I read the book you sent on the way to Steamboat. I really enjoyed it and will wait for a sequel to come out. I'd love to know about what happened when Johnny returned home after the war, your courtship, wedding, etc- It's a great love story! I had no idea that Grandma Schmid is a matchmaker! Johnny sounded like a remarkable man.

Hi Again,

We received Bette's book you mailed to us this afternoon. I had it read cover to cover by 7:00 PM tonight. I have to tell you it was a really heartfelt story to me. (Yes, big brother is a softy at times) Johnny Diedrich was a really good man, a true hero, and I share many of his feelings about our country. (WWII vets, the greatest generation)

Please tell Bette I really enjoyed her book and thanks to her for writing it and signing it so nicely.

I can even further relate to his story by the 45-minute June 1997 flight I took in that B-24 in Chico, CA. One of my great memories. I felt so lucky to even get a chance to ever fly in one.

Thanks you for sending Bette's book sis.

Love, Jose

Contents

About the Author

Bette Regennia Rinker has published poetry, written a health cookbook, and now enjoys sharing with others short novels that she believes will make a difference. She wrote, "SoulMate Warrior" first and was told by Georgia that she believed Regennia was looking for what she had found. She then wrote, "Bombs and Magnolia's" followed by, "A Hero's Love Letters from Stalag III for a Girl Named Georgia." By request she continues to write about this hero's moving love story.

Why I wrote the Story

It is my belief that America can still produce a modern day Abe Lincoln. I am proud to write about this soldier and his love by extreme demand from those who read, "Bombs and Magnolia's" and "A Hero's Love Letters from Stalag Luft III for a Girl Named Georgia." John Diedrich set a standard for anyone who would desire to become the best he or she can be. This is a thank you to him and all soldiers.

I enjoyed writing this story by visualizing it as a stage drama to really emphasis the deep love between Johnny and Georgia as told in his reverie.

Chapter 1

25th Wedding Celebration in Hawaii

Just one look at those beautiful, shimmering seven to eight inch white and gold fish gliding in an ancient effortless manner; and two scrumptious fresh and fruity mi-ties started Georgia laughing so hard that was to become relentless and spiral out of control: A giddiness that comes only with total abandonment.

"Wow! This is a new sensation," Georgia said while her face was becoming more and more rubescent as she pushes her hair off her face and struggles to pull in more air.

Johnny considered for a while, first to himself that they were on a well deserved vacation, and just simply asked, "Would you like another one dear?"

For some reason rolled up in that question was the realization that she had to be...one of the luckiest girl's in the world...the whole of it even. That realization overwhelmed, overtook, and overjoyed her to the extent she could no longer embrace the laughter for herself alone. Tears of joy began to spontaneously flow down her cheeks and hit the highly polished wooden floor. Some dropped between the planks and seemed to make an effortless attempt to rejoin the sea. It was a scene that mesmerized Georgia...completely!

It seemed to her they were glistening like diamonds, just like Johnny's eyes that always lit up for her but even more so now. "I loved that light! In fact that was one of the special reasons....along with many others that had drawn me to him." she added thoughtfully in her magnificent reverie.

Chapter 2

The Old Man with the Torch

Between happy tears for herself and Johnny she could still see the twinkle in his eyes mixed now with a little concern...and for a flash of a moment her mind moved back to Sleetor Hill...one of the first places they had gone together as a couple. Johnny had wanted to show her how the towns all around that hill looked just like starry diamonds below, in the splendor of the night.

The memory of his touch there years ago and his thoughtfulness toward her came flooding back. Then; just as now, never a thought of hurrying home as she was with her love...her Johnny. At least that was what her mind was thinking along with, "Poor Johnny! What on earth am I going to do if I can't stop this uncontrollable laughter?"

In this way the Sand Box restaurant seemed to be much too far away when in reality one had only to stroll through a beautiful winding path decorated with local exotic flowers that were highlighted and skillfully framed by four majestic and regal pillar torches. They were planted stoically in each corner of the garden...just under their room with a graceful ornate piazza and underneath stood another tripod of torches. "If I can just make it to that beautiful gleam underneath our room I will be alright!"

Johnny motioned for her to stand by one of the torches so he could take a picture of her. "See, I still carry a great big torch for you!"

Save not until the shell like conch was blown; this poetical and skillful runner would not budge. It was a custom deeply rooted in the tradition of Hawaiian Minoa. Their citizens believed it to have been established in their annals of times. It seemed to be an integral part of their celebration of life and recognition of gratitude to their creator. Always mindful to keep a light burning into the darkness and the gong of the horn they believed would pierce through to eternity.

Off to the right of them; an even more solemn event was taking place. The moon, now setting, was still giving us some light on the path. The flowers seemed to be tucked in somewhere as the very tip of the moon kissed the mountaintop goodnight in a quiet and reverent way as nature does in its finest moments.

In just as thoughtful a manner, Johnny slid his arm around Georgia's tiny waist. He took his other arm pointing up to the reverent scene at the apex of the mountain to try and distract her from her own overwhelming emotions for her and for him.

In Georgia's heart, there was a place she had buried deep in order to cope with what she realized was the trial of Johnny's life. It was experiences he could never speak of until lately.

While the night mores were looming large in her mind... she could hear Johnny teasing her with his thoughts.

But for her; she wasn't going to let go of Johnny's sacrifice for her, her loved ones and their country. She knew there was a time when he had been on a death march during World War II that he could count a few barley pearls at the bottom of a cup of water. At night when the German guards would go to sleep the soldiers would pillage for roots and literally take the pigs food away from them. They were not pickers, but it literally meant life or death for them. An apology was offered and a prayer.

She knew in her tender heart that there was also a time then when he was so tired and hungry that one foot could barely remember to place itself in front of the other, yet he didn't dare sit down or stop for fear the cold would take him over. There, surprisingly enough, was really no hysteria in the soldiers. Georgia pondered why? Even to this day, this moment.

"Thank God!" she said. Realizing they must have been in touch with their creator: What's best within them.

Here and now she could hear Johnny's voice say to her, "Look, darling, that is where we will go tomorrow. I'll take you to the very top. I read in the paper that there's a great golf course there! Also darling, they have a stand there where people will cut and serve you fresh picked pineapple spears. I'll buy for you all you can eat love."

With that input Georgia remembered coming into their room at the ILIKIA where the staff had placed on the coffee table a huge fresh pineapple wrapped in yellow cellophane. The top was sliced and could be lifted off with several fresh pineapple spears nestled inside. It was such a refreshing thoughtful thing to do. It made one feel sixteen and immortal all over again.

It seemed as if all the world was laughing with them; plus full of light, but for this moment in time the trident laughter, tears, beauty and complete joy was more than Georgia could manage to assimilate.

Finally, arriving to their room on the seventh floor, room seven zero seven, Johnny said, "Georgia, would you like to go out on the balcony to watch the evening's final bow of the day behind the mountain and garden or would you rather take a wink of a nap!"

Without hesitation she said, "Sweetheart, I had better rest for just a bit." as she put her hand to her mouth as if she could stop the giggles.

As she sat down on the edge of the huge round bed in the middle of the room, Johnny hurriedly cleared the way brushing away the perfectly placed lathes and chocolate. The scent of the ginger fern was drifting through the room and the light of the torches were dancing on the ceiling and all around the room. It was such a beautiful dance that was provided by the king of the universe that Georgia, again wispered a quiet apprection.

Johnny cleared Georgia's side of the bed then leaned over to lift her legs to swing them carefully over onto the most comfortable bed in the world.

"That's just right Johnny," Georgia said to him as she watched him head for the balcony...that seemed to beckon him there.

"Thank you," again and again as she tried to yell after him, as she still wrestled to hold the laughter back. The last thing she knew she heard Johnny tell someone below that everything was great! And the thought that Johnny was still as swift as he had ever been which seem to give her a unique comfort.

"Great," she heard again so loud it seemed to echo back to them.

She could see him through the sliding glass door pull up a large beach chair, click it back in position in an effort to see the stars and to get as comfortable as he could, so as to invite the ease of solace that comes when something with awe is stirring one's very soul.

Johnny told her later, "Love, I would have sworn that the old light bearer had come upon the veranda by invitation...I know he took the other padded chair!" Then, Georgia I swear, "he asked me how I and the pretty lady...the very happy lady had gotten to this site...at this point in time...I heard him as clear as day, I did love; I swear it!"

Johnny took notice that the moon was seemingly still for just a moment. Privately he wondered why but didn't linger there as he had so much to share with the old man that seemed so inquisitive.

"If you really want to know," Johnny told him, "It began years ago, so far back that I can barely remember the details, and yet strangely enough, it always seems just like yesterday. Did you ever hear of the old Concord Battle Cry, and ancient ballad? Well, I have one of my own. My version would go like this: Johnny made is voice a little deeper.....

> There was an old bridge that arched over my past and the banners of my mind unfurled. The whole legions of I into battle were cast...with a sigh heard round the world. Now that banner raced over land and sea...seeking creation to girth. It met itself when I met Georgia and I know I had circled the earth...and I did! Then, together we turned with a victory cry, to storm unknown heights. To plant our dream of love high above and beyond the lights...light far greater than those on our first date and drive to Sleeter Hill; but that was when I learned that we did truly trust each other...with a trust that cannot be

measured. Yes, I found in her the greatest of all prizes and one I believe everyone seeks from their cradle to their beyond. It's that great gift of freedom from loneliness, freedom to fly. I believe if one has a true real love relationship, you will never be alone, because in that other person eyes you will always see reflections of yourself. In that other person I believe you will hear your own soul speak. Thus, Georgia can speak for me and likewise, I can speak for her. It was written somewhere in time, when two people leave their parents and cleave to one another those two become as one which rules out alone. See, you know; leave and cleave to one another only."

"This is the key to happiness at least for us, to be free to be without being alone. What do you think? Do you agree, sir?"

"That is why she's so happy...because we are both profoundly happy. This is our twenty fifth year celebration of that declaration. You know it seems like, yesterday we fell in love and, forever, all at the same time. I wish that for you, sir!"

Johnny told him it had been a long journey. One that began years ago, "I cannot pinpoint it now. I do remember shaking my finger at German bombs from the belly of a B24 Bomber. I made a vow then that if I ever made it home again I would protect and follow my dream with everything in me...and that is what I am doing." To the very best of my ability; I believe when you do your best that cancels out all the rest! Do you agree, sir?

As he looked back over his shoulder to make sure the love of his life was settling down, he took notice that she had begun to nibble on a dark chocolate covered macadamia nut...that seemed to relax her. She didn't seem to be aware of him anymore or who he was talking with... And so,

He turned back to the old light bearer and asked, "What is your name? Sorry I didn't ask before."

There were no audible answer. Johnny wanted to tell him so badly just how he had gotten to this point in history...he wanted to recklessly with abandonment step up to the ornate veranda rail just in front him and shout it out to the world.

Would they care? Would they listen? It slowly dawned on Johnny that this story belonged to the world and one he could not hide.

With that in mind, he began to open up to the old man...and with the delight of a child he continued on with his story. Barely audible and with his eyes sort of stalking the last sliver of the moon that seemed to be winking at both of them, Johnny continued on.....

"To make a long story short," he said. "it was twenty five years ago...I packed up my small family on the edge of night. We drove out of Avon, MN in the United States of America; a village, a warm and loving place of about four hundred people...to take them to the most beautiful city on God's green earth. It was out west; to a fast growing metropolis known as Denver, Colorado."

"It was, sir, a dream and a great big promise that I had resolved to keep in the belly of the bomber right over the Poleski Oil Fields."

"To make it short for you...I wanted most of all world peace. Peace was just a dream in the 1940's as the world was becoming closer and closer together due to technology, but no one could predict the fear that would come with it."

"So much to lose they thought. It's amazing to me how everyone was afraid of losing what wasn't even theirs in the first place. The way I see it, we all are just welcome guests here. When our behaviors shake the boundaries of balance...we are out of here anyway...and we get to take with us exactly what we brought in."

"Well anyway, on my ninth mission, after having eight very successful runs my plane got hit...riddled with holes. I gave the command for everyone to bail out. I was the last one to jump out being the officer in charge...the pilot and I. I was a little past 20."

"Even then on my way down my parachute was caught between wind and fire. Even though it seemed an angel carried me out of harms way...my stomach was doing a number on me anyway. Miraculously I thought of this lovely lady." He pointed back with his thumb as he usually did. It was then that I remembered my last evening at her mother's house; how she had made me feel just to look at her...and how her mother welcomed me in with open arms. In fact, it was by her invitation that I was there. Those memories completely soothed my mind...just as they still do today.

Georgia's Father, whom plays violin.

If you really want to know let me tell you what that beautiful intelligent lady in there set aside for me. She was born in Avon, Minnesota, population four hundred, surrounded by many lakes and forest. She lived above her father's store in an eleven room home. The towns' telephone company was down the hall...a kind of mini version mall and her name is "Georgia."

Her mother, Veronica, had been a printer in Minneapolis, Minnesota. She was introduced to Georgia's Dad by his brother...who owned a shoe store and needed a partner for a dance. Even though it was forty miles from Avon, he would drive to see her on the weekends. Soon they were married.

Veronica relinquished her own ambitions to make what seemed to be the perfect home with three beautiful girls. Veronica's life evolved completely around George and her three girls, after Veronia and Georgis's marriage. There was no question she felt and acted as though her life was fulfilled.

How do I know you ask! She created a peace in that home one could not stay away from.

Her big brown eyes were sparkling and could pierce right through a person. They could just cut to the chase if you know what I mean.

After Veronica and George's marriage he drove her to Chicago, Illinois on a huge shopping spree to furnish their home. She selected beautiful dark Queen Ann furniture... throughout the house; special wall papers to set it off and, of course, she loved her chandeliers...all crystal throughout the home.

Chapter 3

Georgia's Music Premeates Through Town

S he also had a grand piano sent to that address...shipped all the way back to Avon. It didn't take long under her care to turn that home into a modern day palace. One that took on the air that a king and queen would be comfortable with...and they were one in our eyes...and to anyone that knew them. Especially since their great love of each other and their many talents were there.

I loved their home and Georgia did too. There were always wonderful aroma's coming from the kitchen. Often, I took her fish and just as often I was invited over for my favorite meal of roast beef, vegetables cooked slowly with a bay leaf and Worcestershire sauce. That's the best of life, good food, good company!

Georgia said she could practice piano all she wanted at least an hour every day and look down the main street always aware of what was going on. She was watching me from those windows long before I knew her...even though it did feel as though someone was aware of me.

And so; in this place with her mother's tender care and guidance, Georgia prepared herself for a great future. She was preparing to be a professional Broadway dancer and music teacher. Our meeting changed all that as he turned to emphasize that point by looking the old man straight in the eyes; eyes so bright it was hard to see them clearly.

Just like her mother, she was capable of putting all of her ambitions aside to embellish my life and our five children. You know, sir if one is loved you feel safe, secure, valued and appreciated...that brings all the happiness in the world. All that one will ever need; that is exactly what she brings to me.

Great outfits

Chapter 4

Never Regreted Pulling Out of Town

S he decorated our lives in too many ways to enumerate here and now I'll never be able to thank her in equal measure. This vacation is one of the ways I wanted to say "thank you" to her...I have other ways you know. I thank her in any way I can think up...my appreciation knows no boundaries. All this brought out that wonderful twinkle in his eyes.

Harmoniously, Georgia's music would permeate effortlessly down the stairs throughout the store...then drift through, melodically, through the streets. I, myself, heard it but tried not to let it spellbound me...now; that was hard to do; Johnny said, with laughter!

I remember on Sunday's and after the family meal together Georgia; her father would say, "Come on Georgia, you play the piano and I'll play violin and sing for my family that I adore." And thank you Veronica [that would be her mother], for that lovely meal.

He would put the violin under his arm and sing in a mélange of soft, yet a strong voice, his favorite arias. I'll tell you, he was every bit as handsome as Rudolph Valentino...but I never did hear Rudolf bellow out the love songs like Dad. He realized he had something to sing about!

George sang in the church choir for fifty years. In his eighty sixth year on Sunday he had dressed up in his black suit; not the one he worked in every day but similar. He put on a crisp, perfectly ironed shirt, went down the stairs, got out the door then turned around to lock it and just fell over with a massive heart attack. He never came out of that deep sleep but I can tell you this much...He was surrounded completely by love and happiness. He lacked absolutely nothing.

I'll tell you sir, I wanted to have a life like he built...or even be like him. I would often spend long hours talking with him in the store and on our deliveries for the store. I would pick his brain, I would think to myself, "I love this man!" I never did get to tell him but I tell him now in many ways, especially taking care of his and my Georgia.

Slowly and surely, I became aware of his warm and genuine manner. I saw him as one of the most brilliant men I knew for his family, his village, and "that" we know has a way of permeating into the world.

I know he would have preferred that we stay in Avon and take over the bank and help in the General Store, but Georgia and I both had a dream of seeing the world; of pursuing aspirations of our own.

Therefore, as hard as it was, we slowly and reluctantly pulled away from that idyllic world. A world that anymore would put up a fight to maintain. Now, we could reach the goal that I had set for myself in the belly of that B24 Bomber and that Georgia had dreamed of as a child.

Johnny came to the realization years ago with bullets and bombs hitting his war plane that life is designed for the connoisseur of living; that all the parts and pieces are there, but it is up to the individuals ingenuity to put the puzzle of life successfully together...and if one gets lucky... finds an honorable help mate...all the better...all the easier.

I don't know if one could call it luck that fate would have the mother of your mate love you also as Veronica did me. She told Georgia when we did pull away from Avon to never come home without "Johnny," that's me! As he straightend up a bit and his chest swelled.

Hesitating a moment to ponder if it was luck or destiny...or did one actually create or etch out his own character moment by moment, day by day, year by year or was there a power greater than ourselves operating constantly that when one is capable of yielding to it could actually whittle one right into eternity?

Well, Johnny vowed to himself not to bore the old man with his vacation reveries but when he looked over the torch bearer seemed to be given arrested attention to the details so much so that he felt compelled now to answer him as though he was an interlocutor and the motion was made for details.

Hence, Johnny repeated the question back to himself..."just how did Georgia and I get here to this point in time in Hawaii; her laughing her heart out and me sitting here talking with the local torch bearer; their keeper of time; which ironically keeps no record of time either.

This created a stir in Johnny's mind...so all the afore mentioned memories went racing through his head again. Then, favorite national parks... favorite conventions would cry out to be mentioned...there was a hesitation; and then a chuckle of sorts that commanded the old man's attention.

I remember the time I took her to Vale, Colorado on a vacation for her and a convention for me. After meeting the guys liked to play poker up town. Our wives were free to do as they wished.

This particular night we both arrived at our suite at the same time...around two or three in the morning. She began to tell me all the girls loved the band in one of the nearby dance halls. She said the hall was elegant with blonde oak floors and red drapes, red padded chairs, and tables that sat on graduated tiers. They were on a lower one so they could watch the dancers.

She told me also it was so much fun they were going again the next night. I couldn't let her have that much fun by herself so I bowed out of the poker game, even though I was winning, and joined my wife; a better win; I considered.

We danced every dance. She wore her deep red china suit that I had bought for her; it made her look as though she owned the place. She turned down all invitations to dance only wanting to dance with me and I felt likewise.

However; snow had begun to fall; I suggested we head back to our room at the hotel. We decided to walk; as we did, the streets had begun to freeze over. Pretty soon we started sliding and skating down the street singing the Blue Danube Waltz. La de da de da. Consequently; we were a little too loud; the people began to come out on their balconies looking down at us to see who it was having too much fun.

Another one of our memorable times and was along the lines of a gravamina; I guess you could call it. The song of the Hawaiian bird the OO could be heard in the distance, but neither man turned to find where the birds paean call came from...there was just rapt attention to know more about Georgia.

Therefore Johnny proceeded on to say, "One of the cutest things she did was the time we went to visit her parents as we always did every summer. It was unusually hot that day... Georgia and her sisters and mother were busy preparing a feast for us.

My brother in law, Pete, was an FBI man with loads of news for a guy. He suggested we drive to the Little Alcove Bar and Restaurant to catch up on the news...this was sometimes his habit and her sister would be home along with the eight children. It didn't sit well with Georgia. In fact, it pained her a lot.

Well; this particular hot and muggy summer when we were there...somehow our quick drink ran into Georgia's mothers' elegant dinner time. Consequently, we had lingered just a little too long. So Georgia with her fear of making her mother angry wanted to make sure that it didn't become a habit...I guess it just hit her wrong! That prompted her to just start walking about a mile down the hot paved highway in her bare feet and traveling just as fast as her pretty little legs would take her!

The next thing I knew she was standing in the door of the bar yelling, "Johnny! Dinner's ready!"

My back was to her but when I turned around there she was in all her glory...nothing on except a regal red bathing suit. I never told her but she did take my breath away!

But the kicker was, I heard this awful sound as though someone had just gotten slapped. I turned back around to check...sure enough it was my own beautiful Georgia who had just taken a swipe at the local "plain clothing" sheriff. She just quickly swirled around and hi-tailed it back home.

I let her walk the distance. She told me later she, at least, knew that had it been me...it would have cost her a divorce. Instead, when I regained my focus; I estimated the offense and the cost as judge and jury; I apologized to the red faced man; laid money down...he pushed it away and asked me not to worry about it...as it had just woke him up and he needed to be home himself; but, Pete and me turned and left every bit as quickly as Georgia. The case was closed.

I never told her this, but it just amazed me how beautiful she looked standing in the doorway of that little out of the way place. I, in truth, wanted an exit from there and always believed she must have read my mind. I learned that day that colorful exits are just as good as any.

Thus, I did show up just in time. George, my wife's father, never realized how close he had come to having his own daughter come before him as the Justice of the Peace. It was never brought up again. I loved that about her. She would just tell you once, never nagging.

We learned to express ourselves and if we didn't agree, we would walk away from each other...mull over what the other had thought and expressed, then we would come to a reasonable understanding, a far better one than before. A selfless one that makes one happier in the end. In fact, each is elated that the other one tried to comprehend a little different approach to life's situations.

It's been my observation that selfishness has no boundaries...no end. "Do you know what I mean?" When you really love someone as much as I love her; that, lady in there...that love truly washes over all that. That love will tell you exactly what to do if you really think it through.

You see, sir, I have never been afraid to ask myself what role did I play in creating a misunderstanding or an uneasy situation that I wasn't exactly comfortable with. Invariably, I was just as unreasonable as she was and many times more so. But that would only make me love her more because with her love I was forced to grow.

I enjoyed taking her with me on many tours around America. I wanted her to stay in the best places, because she was born on a silver platter; yet, not wasteful. She managed to put everything to good use.

Her mother taught her that broken eggs make the best sour cream cookies and ripe bananas the best divine banana bread. The flour sacks made each family member a beautiful mattress pad.

She earned the best in her way...all that life had to offer and I took great pleasure in watching her light up at new ideas and events. Her gratitude makes her stand out from the rest...and her stately manner; and just as many times I would whisper a "thank you" to myself to her mother Veronica for creating my girl, my Georgia.

You know twenty four seven Georgia's main concern was her family and home. She was very good at it... of course to me she was the best. In fact, she was very professional like her mother Veronica. I'm sorry, sir, time lines run together for me, but as near as I can remember our first home was on Reed Street.

Georgia had left her home town and life as she knew it and all that it held for her...never ever to bring it up again to me. I did always appreciate that; more than I could tell her.

As far as I know we never regretted pulling out of Avon. Of course, we missed our family and life-long friends there but we felt we were carrying them right along with us in our minds and in our hearts.

Thank God, we both wanted the same things in our life's adventures! We wanted to see the world instead of just a slice of it there in our town. To have many different experiences was our goal...to become broad-minded.

I'll tell you right here and now, it was really enough. All that anyone could ever dream of...but we had the opportunity to chase our dreams. That is exactly what we did. We loved every minute of it.

Look! look up there!!! see those two love birds flying... see how free they are. That is precisely what Georgia and I did. Birds teach us a lot you know, as he reflected on a tiny sparrow that had landed right in front of him on the banister. It stared right into Johnny's eyes as if to understand. No one moved a muscle!

Chapter 5

Enter Georgia: Johnny Thought.

Fom out of nowhere; He would do more sports but he would rather be with me," Georgia chimed in. "Don't forget to tell him dear that we gave up a lot of things so all the children could go to college."

Johnny interrupted her by adding, "She would only buy what we needed; didn't have many visitors and didn't visit around herself."

Those were my only two requests upon marrying her. She taught the children the morals to see them through; this good character brought them the best of friends and they were welcomed anywhere.

"Georgia," tell him, our listener, about our five children.

"They," she added, "were already on softball teams and football teams; of which they were usually the captains (like their father). Johnny started playing sports with them as soon as they could throw a ball or a fishing line.

We would try to live in areas where other children were engaged in life. We purposely enrolled them in Christian Brothers High School to be with goal oriented company. They were well behaved, never detractingly rowdy.

My oldest son John was the only one born in Avon and moved with us to Denver. When he grew up he would go by and pick up Danny Hamilton because his mother was alone. In reverse, Mike and Pat Farley had only one son so they would pick up Dan and Tad for school and its activities.

Then, when we moved to Reed Street, the girl next door to grandpa's would pick up Gi Gi and Paul. We all helped each other. They went to school with all the productive kids in town so naturally they were on Golf teams and in Hockey games. They did so well that Tad was driven all over the region in a big white limousine to compete in golf.

Gi Gi, my daughter, had a friend who was from Germany. They were very affluent and owned a condominium in Vale. They would often invite her to go with them there when she wasn't going with us to Avon and mainly National parks.

We wanted them to appreciate the history of the United States; but also to love nature and to be able to entertain themselves without a lot of money. This helping spirit that evolved out of these experiences seemed to move all of us into the right place. Much of these spectacular events were happening when we lived on Broadmore Street.

Johnny soon accepted a position is Cheyenne, Wyoming at First Wyoming Bancorp. First, he was hired to be head of the Investment Department and moved on to clean up the Trust Department. So when the President resigned, I told him to apply for that position as he was the most qualified. He had prepared himself by going to summer school and flying to New York to graduate. He took me to the best plays and restaurants there as sort of a graduation party.

The bond people in Denver also referred him for the position saying he was conservative, honest and above all ethical. That was in the Capital; so; we were invited to all political affairs and actually went to the state officer's homes for dinners. I guess one of my favorites was Jackson Hole State Banquet held on Lake Moran overlooking the Grand Tetons.

Chapter 6

Johnny' Came to Realize Years Ago... In this Soldier's Heart

Benlythgoe   Teddy   Jordan

2nd row Jeff Georgia & Erin Johnny & Kate Lythgoe James

3rd row Joey Tad Samantha Kate Viann

4th row Paul Richlythgoe & Gigi Dan John

Johnny & Georgia 50th Wedding Annv.
John & Vians 25th Wedding Annv.
We celebrated together in Denver at Clubhouse in John's area
Johnny & I sewed the dress for Lil Kate.
Dan's 2 big boys Nate & Daniel in Mich Univ.
John's daughter Julie was in Colo. Univ.

This is where Johnny became President of seventeen banks. So he decided on one of those occasions that he wanted to be north of town. He, then bought us ten acres and had a brand new red brick home built. It was a complete ranch life with pot lucks often with the neighbors. He had moved a long way from the cabin by the creek, that he used to bathe in and wind and rain blowing through the windows. Just like Abe!!!

We bought for Paul, our youngest child, on his birthday a beautiful Palomino Quarter horse, and a gigantic trailer. Johnny built a stall for the hay and to shelter the horses. By eleven years old Paul was totally involved in ranching.

One of the neighboring ranchers by the name of Mr. Reese would hire Paul and another friend to help him on his ranch. He would pull weeds and clean stalls, fix fences and come home at supper time. So to that extent, Paul majored in farm and ranch management in a nearby college.

Thinking back at Molly Christian High School they had created what was a replica of a royal court that constituted a king and queen. So, John, my first son was appointed to be king of that epic on St. Patrick's Day for the parade. I was determined not to miss him as his float went by; hence I got the worst sunburn of my life. It didn't matter as long as I was able to see his float and naturally I was bursting with pride.

It makes a good memory that his friend Doug Hamilton volunteered son John to escort his cute cousin to the high school prom...luckily he had a blast and then the Mullens that lived out near Stapleton Airport had a daughter that also asked John to escort her to their Prom. He, in turn, asked her to go to his. Then the president of the student council needed an escort to her Prom and asked John. He was so pleased he could use that tuxedo so much and get his money's worth. When in reality he thought it would be the opposite. He had a great time as far as I know.

At about the end of college for John he met his match and fell in love with a petite dark-haired beauty named ViAnn.

He ran mostly with a group of boys, so I didn't know anything about her until he said, "Mom, could I bring my girlfriend home for Thanksgiving dinner?" She brought her sister with her for that first meeting.

I learned she had worked her way through college. Her folks had let her brothers run the farm in Nebraska so they could move to Greeley to claim residence. They bought a motel and hired ViAnn to help keep the rooms clean.

It just brought back the memory of my own father, who for all his life, from sixteen on; would put on black pants, a starched white dress shirt and a black tie to open the store every morning at five thirty. He'd come upstairs only for lunch and dinner. Sunday was always reserved for church and the choir until the Sunday he stood there waiting (as Johnny said) for his grandson to pick him up for church as he could no longer walk there. The grandson found him with his Bible and songbook laying by the door with just a look of peace on his face. I suppose he had left his violin at home that day. Almost like he knew he wouldn't need it.

My mother had died ten years before Daddy. After that he just simplified his life by using paper plates, towels and cups. He seemed lonely though and didn't want to sing as much.

He kept the store running as smoothly as he could under those conditions. Daddy said she had taken the pills for diabetes; and that had caused the hardening of the arteries that killed her.

She loved chocolate and caramel ice cream from the store. She would say, "this is so, so good!"

I would tell her, "Mom, you shouldn't eat so much." But she would reply just as fast, "Oh Georgia, I'll just take my pill."

Meanwhile; Daddy and Johnny would deliver farm fresh eggs all over the county. Their favorite treat was to always stop at Braak and Erbrechins for their hot beef sandwiches served with fresh course horse radish. They loved listening to other news in surrounding towns; and the stories they were so eager to share."

Chapter 7

About the Horn of the Moon

....The Moonlight Glow By Now Well

Suited This Spectacular Scene

I t was now about the horn of the moon; but Georgia was not yet ready to stop her loquacity. With enthusiasm she remembered wonderful times, full of joy for her. Her mouth began to water as she remembered those giant cashews that Johnny would always bring to her from Fanny Farmers store on these runs.

"It's a beautiful memory," she reflected, "Johnny could build the brightest memories. Yes, that is what he is...a perfect memory builder. It stirs me every time...even now."

Now the last two weeks in June of every year we would load up our family in our, what we called a General Sherman tank, better known as a big white Chevy station wagon, and head for Mom and Dad's home in Avon; Minnesota that is! We packed our food as no one wanted to stop for anything.

The children could not wait to get to Joy's house to jump back in the Middle of Avon Lake. Joy's family lived in a little cottage there with a porch. It was the western side of the lake...nestled in tall elegant pine trees that Minnesota is noted for. It was a picture!

I would sit there and watch the kids with my feet in the air...just like him...as she seemingly points to Johnny.

The houses there were only used for summer vacations. So much of the time we had this beautiful recreation site to ourselves...and the environment was very much like this one. It was, and this is, the essence vital part of the spirit... needful ingredients to make a completed soul I would say.

The children felt this balance and harmony that was there; so I would just sit there and watch them run around as children do...in and out of Joy's walk out basement. From the patio, I could see very clear as they floated near me on their inner tubes; splashing and playing as though there were no civil law here; only pledges of silent honor. Seals of fate that only a higher power could produce; what more could there be! But Johnny was always capable of producing more...look at us now in wonderment!

I say this with the greatest of humility, sir. I soon learned that my precious daughter Gi Gi was much like a gorgeous belle with beauty of form and movement as graceful as an elegant bird. She is a beneficent gift to any one in her life and a light to be admired. The benison of knowing her had added to my life more than I can say.

Her brother's understood that and always treated her with the greatest respect.

However, I did observe that beautiful, rich and smart was a problem for her when she would have to move to a new home…a new area. Kris Pringle knew this all too well as she was in the same position. Lucky for them, they could compete with the best of them. It was fun to watch them overcome!

College brought for Gi Gi the suitor of her life. Rick was studying computer science and was an ex-Marine. I think it was pretty much love at first sight for them. They seem to be completely comfortable together.

Georgia hesitated for only a moment with a deep sigh; she looked out of the corner of her eye to see if she still had the old light bearer's attention.

"That leaves only Dan and Kate," she said a little louder. Dan was captain also of the football team. He also received a scholarship to attend Notre Dame University. It's one of the best in the States; one has to be really bright to go there and keep up.

This little shy Irish-German girl named Kate was attending St. Mary's College across the street. They both were drawn to the arts and met each other at an art class.

She told me she had actually first laid eyes on him when he was nonchalantly riding an old bicycle near the college. She learned he had retrieved that old bike out of the dump along with an old Denver Post bag he had retrieved also; they both were cleaned and repaired and just like new. She said she thought, "Well he looks interesting!" That special look of a special man and woman led to their marriage. For some reason son Tad and his wife and daughter wanted to be out of the loop. Georgia winked and disappeared somewhere.

The moonlight glow by now well suited this spectacular scene. It bathed and nudged Johnny's pensive thoughts to a higher pinnacle. It flashed through his consideration that even if he had all the power in the world to freeze this glistening moment...he would not!

Then, almost thinking out loud he said, "I know in this soldiers heart; with my lady there, pointing sideways with his whole hand now, with her the very best will always be right out in front of us...that's her amazing way!

Speaking of my girl, "Where did she go? Where is the old man with the torch? Johnny shook his head as if to wake up or at least to comprehend what was unfolding to him...when he realized that by now he was unusually hungry for that T-bone steak and lobster dinner. That was just a few feet away; where those shimmering fish that kept no record of time as if in tune with the light bearer and the ocean could be seen and felt as one dined.

Still somewhat mesmerized; he hurriedly found Georgia amid the chocolate and flowers, seemingly, asleep on the bed. He leaned over to nudge her awake with a passionate and profound kiss. Ever so gentle he helped her swing her legs off the bed.

Arm in arm they headed for the garden path that lead to the renowned Sand Box Restaurant. The birds seemed happy also as they chirped now more softly than before what seemed to be an evening love song. The most beautiful they had ever heard them chirp!

Johnny and Georgia took note that the all colorful exotic flowers were swaying as if to keep time with that song and with the perpetual breeze drifting up from the sea.

"Let's just take is easy love, it's our time," he told Georgia and so as not to alert her of his own curiosity about the old light bearer. He would turn his head ever so easy from time to time...wanting desperately to thank him for being such a good listener. However, he was nowhere to be found!

"Oh well," Johnny thought. We will carry him with us in our hearts. He pulled Georgia as close as he could to whisper in her ear, "Darling, hearts are all that matter!"

Then, with a slightly more audible voice he told her this, "When morning breaks on this very path, I promise you Georgia that we'll make the best memory like no other memories have ever been and if I'm successful the honor of loving you will stretch into forever.

The light flickered and then stood still as if to embrace this perfect moment that would forever make its way into eternity.

Johnny simply added, "You'll see, my love." When morning breaks on this very path, I promise you Georgia...

...That we'll make the most extraordinary memories that have ever been and if I'm successful the honor of loving you will stretch into forever.

Chapter 8

Letters and Collections of Photos from Georgia's Scrapbook

Georgia was just told by Johnny "See, I still carry a big torch for you."

The Ilikai where Johnny and Georgia stayed.

The delicious pineapple mentioned

The beginning of something big!

Georgia watering her mother's garden.

The candid camera catches one of the piano groups playing the Schubert-Bauer "Rondo Brilliant," the violists bowing Bach's "Sarabande" under the baton of H. R. Waugh of St. Cloud, (below) eleven-year-old Gorga Vern Schmid of Avon closely attending Director James Sample in the Mozart-Maier "Andante and Minuet."

Georgia said at one point the keys seem to play by themselves.

Georgia said at one point the keys seem to play by themselves.

SHERATON
MAUI
HOTEL

Georgia was just told by Johnny "See, I still carry a big torch for you."

The Ilikai where Johnny and Georgia stayed.

The delicious pineapple mentioned

Settling in

The balcony at the Illikai

Georgia holding the pineapple in this beautiful scene.

The profile of Georgia's Father, GEORGE.

The variety store Georgia lived above.

Georgia's fathers office

ILIKAI
SHERATON
MAUI
HOTEL

Flying into Hawaii for our wedding anniversary

The Beginning

The End

"What the caterpillar calls the end of the world...the butterfly calls the beginning.

Johnny and Georgia's first date.

The Diedrich's back porch where Johnny proposed.

You've taken a place

centered in my being

there you sit

on a silver throne

vibrant, radiant influence

on most everything

balance of eternity

neither one alone

I glow within

lite from your spirit

reflect sweet harmony tendrils of love

impart peace to our being

what else to say

I love you, Georgia

I love you!

Dear Georgia   May 9, 1944

My way of living has changed suddenly due to the fact of being shot down on one of our missions a while back. Am a P.O.W. now. We are allowed only one parcel each sixty days. Certain items are restricted. I wrote Mother a few days ago and informed her what I needed most. But I can receive any amount of letters. Would you please send me some photos of yourself. Say hello to your Mother and family. I wonder just how long it will before we can go bowling again. I hope by Christmas at least. We are allowed to write two letters and four cards, missing you, love Johnny

Kriegsgefangenenlager   Datum: May 25, 1944

Dear Georgia,
Am looking forward to see you one of these days, darling. Forgive the repetitions but don't forget your photo. Am still getting along all right. Missing you always, love Johnny

Kriegsgefangenenlager   May 25; 1944

Dear Georgia,

Am looking forward to see you one of these days, darling. Forgive the repetitions but don't forget your photo. Am still getting along all right. Missing you always, love Johnny

Dearest Georgia   Sept. 30, 1944

How quickly ones pace of life changes. Yesterday and days before were so dull and empty today the sun was shinning brightly even though the sky was cloudy. Georgia, darling, never have I received such a beautiful letter as yours is. It has made this day the happiest I have known as a "Krugie." One minute you are in your glory enjoying every bit of what American freedom stands for - happiness! As a P.O.W. there is nothing to do but "sweat out" events, hearsays, and rumors. Stare through and at the fence, walk within the confined borders, discuss past experiences and plans for the future. Missing you, darling, more than you know! Love Johnny

Dearest Georgia,   **October 16, 1944**

If there are more than seven heavens I was in it all day. Talk about sweet letters, Georgia, honey, I received one from you today. My thoughts were lying in a triangular array. Home, Georgia, and how long will "it" be? Your letter was strictly dessert in the line of brain food and dreams. I drooled at the mooth when you mentioned strawberry short cake. Went on my first parole walk this afternoon. Was notified to the extent that there was a personal parcel in the outer lager for me. I would get it either Saturday or Monday. No, sugar, we don't hear American broadcasts. Have been spending most of my time reading in the ref. library and accumulating material for a wartime log. Tell me about the church celebration. You're letters are everything, Love Johnny

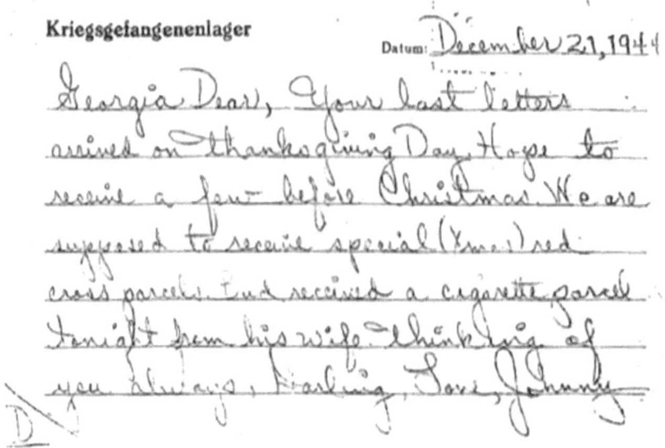

Kriegsgefangenenlager   December 21, 1944

Georgia Dear, Your last letter arrived on Thanksgiving Day. Hope to receive a few before Christmas. We are supposed to receive special (Xmas) red cross parcel. Bud received a cigarette parcel tonight from his wife. Thinking of you always, Darling, Love, Johnny

Dearest Georgia,   November 13, 1944

Each letter from you, darling, definitely brings more and more happiness into my restricted life. My reason for craving snapshots so, is for present state of affairs, it is the closest we can be to one another. I hope the sisters won't be too angry with me for cluttering up their main parlor more than their want. What subject's have you taken up this semester? On my return to the states I intend to get my share of walking in the woods, skating, fishing, hunting, bowling, and dancing, if you wish, with you, Georgia, darling, to strains of beautiful, slow, sweet music. You'll have a big job teaching me all over again. I shouldn't be dreaming out loud. The parcel in which you enclosed your snapshots arrived on Oct. 26 in perfect shape. Thank you, Georgia you are as beautiful as ever. The one of you in the white suit makes me weak in the knees. You may write letters with envelopes if you wish. I'd prefer those to the forms, then you can enclose snapshots. Say hello to everyone maybe I'll be dropping in for a visit soon. Bye darling, thinking of you day and night. Don't practice bowling too much! Love always, Johnny

Georgia Dear,												December 13, 1944

It is surprising how difficult these letters are becoming to write. Yet it shouldn't be that way. If it wouldn't be for your sweet letters and especially the snapshots I'd go beserk. They afford me the only real happiness I have here. My log book is very near complete as it ever will be. So when a good book comes into the room it makes the rounds of the sergeants we now have. Our lot here is simply an opportunity for self improvement and development. Every moment spent reading is sort of a Triumph. The other day we started an inter-room bridge and pinochle tournament. Kes and I are in first place in bridge. Did I ever mention that we took first place in the volley ball tournament in the sergeants' league? We are working to do the same in basketball. This afternoon we were very fortunate winning the THIRD game this season. I know that I am an unbearable pest, darling, but please send a photo of yourself as soon as possible. I have a very special reason! Missing you Georgia, more than you know, love Johnny

GEORGE

The wedding banquet at St. Cloud Country Club in 1946.
Daddy had opened after the war.

Johnny and little brothers big catch in Avon Lake.

The honeymoon at Daluth's Lake Superior in
Minnesota.

The Wedding
The Dream

Georgia,

I Loved the book — it has helped me make a decision to do an action at Work. I thoroughly relaxed after reading your book Sunday after the hot mineral bath. Your buddy, Judy

Thanks again for the gift.

Ms. Georgia Diedrich

First date first kiss
Courtship
Johnny asked me to go to Calif. with them.
Went for lots of rides on the country roads through the wooded hills. The large tall trees were were reaching up high + over the road entwining their branches it looked like a cathedral

AVON
CORNET

B.R. RINKER

DIEDRICH

Elmer John Diedrich, Jr., 77, a resident of T-or-C for the past 15 years, passed away Tuesday, February 29, 2000, in his home. He was born in Los Angeles, California, August 17, 1922, the son of Elmer John Diedrich, Sr. and Helen Leitner Diedrich.

After enlisting with the United States Army Air Corps during World War II, he was stationed in Italy where he received an air medal. While serving his country, he was a prisoner of war in Germany for one year and eight days.

Having graduated from the University of St. John's in Minnesota with a degree in business administration, he became a banker in Denver, Colorado, a position he held for the next 40 years. During his career, he found time to teach banking in the Junior Achievement Program and Investments at the Colorado Banking School at Colorado University. He subsequently attended graduate school at Rogers University and became president of American Heritage Bank in Colorado Springs, Colorado. He later became president of the First Wyoming Bank Corporation in Cheyenne, Wyoming. The Optimists, Kiwanis and Rotary Club benefited from his efforts during these years.

In retirement, he enjoyed golfing, fishing, wood working and quilting.

Johnny Diedrich is honored here

★ TRUTH OR CONSEQUENCES, NEW MEXICO ★
VETERANS
MEMORIAL PARK &
HAMILTON
MILITARY MUSEUM
Santa Fe
25
Albuquerque
25
Truth or Consequences
Exits 75 & 79
Las Cruces
El Paso
2.5-hr drive from Albuquerque on I-25 S
2-hr drive from El Paso on I-25 N
For additional visitor information & attractions visit
www.sierracountynewmexico.info
VETERANS MEMORIAL PARK &
HAMILTON MILITARY MUSEUM
996 South Broadway
Truth or Consequences, NM 87901
TheWall@windstream.net
www.torcveteransmemorial.com
575.894.0750
575.740.7111

WELCOME TO THE TRUTH OR CONSEQUENCES VETERANS MEMORIAL PARK AND
THE HAMILTON MILITARY MUSEUM. THE PARK IS DEDICATED TO THE MEMORIES OF
FAMILY AND FRIENDS THAT HAVE DEDICATED THEIR LIVES TO THE SERVICE OF OUR
GREAT COUNTRY. WE ENCOURAGE ALL GENERATIONS TO COME AND EXPERIENCE
THE "WALL THAT HEALS" AS WELL AS OTHER ATTRACTIONS WITHIN THE PARK.

VIETNAM MEMORIAL WALL

In February 2001 a half scale traveling replica of the world renown Vietnam Veterans Memorial Wall made its permanent home in Truth or Consequences, New Mexico. This wall was one of a handful of wall replicas traveling throughout the nation. Since its inception in 1996, more than one million people have visited the Memorial Funds Traveling Wall exhibition. It has made stops in nearly 200 U.S. locales in addition to touring the four Provinces of Ireland. This wall, that was purchased by New Mexico with the assistance of local businessmen traversed the United States for approximately three years until being retired in December 2002.

"The Wall That Heals speaks not only to the loss, but of the lives of 58,420 men and women named on the wall — our parents, children, neighbors and friends" said Jan C. Scruggs, founder and president of the Vietnam Veterans Memorial Fund. We are confident that the memorial will become a frequent visiting place for those honoring the service of all who served in Vietnam and in particular, the 399 New Mexicans who made the ultimate sacrifice. This memorial in Truth or Consequences serves as a common gathering place for New Mexicans both young and old to show respect and honor in rememberence.

WALK OF EDUCATION

Take a historical walk along a congressional Medal of Honor shaped path and read our country's history on a monument representing each conflict the United States has been involved in since 1775 up to and including Afghanistan and Iraq.

HAMILTON MILITARY MUSEUM

Through the generous donations of men and women who have served and their families in the armed forces, this museum and it's contents are a living memorial and history of our country and the dedication of those who served. This is their story. Depicted are just some of the many rare and educational exhibits within the museum that are continuously being updated and expanded.

British Admiral
Napoleonic Wars
1800-1815

U.S. Army Staybright
Iraq War
2004-2009

★ IN THE TRUEST SENSE, FREEDOM CANNOT BE BESTO

Handmade knife by soldier during WW1 - 1918 US Marine Corps
West wing of the Hamilton Military Museum
State of New Mexico
Distinguished Service Medal
WWII SILVER STAR WINNER
Sergeant Lewis Cain
1942 Hot Springs
High School Graduate
1911A1 .45 caliber Colt
Standard WWII issue
Seaman 2nd Class Dionald Wessels
Served 1942-1945
Boots worn in the Vietnam War
Pete Padilla Collection
Sierra County, NM local
1 star General Strong's
BDU Uniform
2 star General Smith's
1984 Class A Dress Uniform
Buffalo Soldier - 9th Cavalry Regiment
Active 1866-1950
VED, IT MUST BE ACHIEVED ~ FRANKLIN D. ROOSEVELT ★

www.ingramcontent.com/pod-product-compliance
Lightning Source LLC
Chambersburg PA
CBHW021332060726
47591CB00006B/1985